And No Nobody Likes Me

Written by Lisa Rajan

Illustrated by Amit Tayal

Collins

1 I don't like times tables

Finally! I'm on the last question … 8 × 7. What is it? Hmm … that's a hard one. Is it 48? Or 58? 56? Urgh. I don't know. And I don't really care.

I just want to go out to play, before all the best snow is gone. Everyone else went out ages ago. They'll all be throwing snowballs and building snowmen already.

"Finish all the questions before you go out to play, Carrie," says Ms Ali.

I'm good at most of the other times tables, but the seven times table is really hard. I don't know how anyone can work out the answers without counting on their fingers. Kesha can do it, though.

Kesha is my best friend in the whole world and she's really good at all the times tables, even sevens and eights.

She's really good at everything actually. And she's very funny and good at making things.

I bet she's making some good snowballs right now. I want to make some too!

"I'm just finishing the last sum, Ms Ali!" I say.

I wish Kesha hadn't run out to play as soon as she was done. She would know the answer. I bet she put 58. I'm going to put that. There … 58. Finished!

Where's my coat? I can't see it. Everyone charged outside in such a hurry.

I can't find it. But who cares if it's cold? There's snow to play with! Kesha and I will build a snowman together. A really big one. And make snow angels.

Right. I can go outside, finally. Where's Kesha?

We always play together at breaktime. Always.
She usually waits for me and we go outside together, but
I saw her run off as soon as she was finished.

Why was she in such a hurry? Was it the snow or
something else? Was she trying to get away from me?

I can't see her anywhere. Is she hiding from me? I bet
she is.

2 Zara doesn't like me

"Have you seen Kesha?" I ask Uma.

"Over there, by the tree," says Uma, pointing.

Kesha is talking to someone. I can't really see who
it is. She's got her head down. Is it … Is it … Zara?
The new girl? She started at the beginning of term, a few
weeks ago. Kesha doesn't really know her. Why would
Kesha talk to Zara?

Zara is shaking her head. Why is she doing that?
Kesha must have asked her a question. What would
she ask? Was it a question about me?

I bet it was. I bet Kesha just asked Zara if she likes me.
And Zara said no. That's not very nice of her.

Now Kesha is shaking her head. She doesn't like
me either? Neither of them likes me!

Why don't they like me? What have I done?

Zara doesn't even know me, and Kesha is supposed to be my best friend.

Supposed to be. Hmm …

I know what's happening!

Kesha must want a new best friend. She doesn't like me anymore. She thinks I'm stupid and boring. She wants Zara to be her new best friend.

Kesha has probably been hoping someone new would come to our school for ages, so that she could stop being friends with me and make a new friend instead.

Kesha wants to be friends with someone fun and nice and normal and clever. Someone who is always happy and smiley and won't ask for help with the spellings every week. Or the seven and eight times tables.

Zara finished both sides of the times tables test before I'd even turned the page over. She was so fast. So she was the first one to pack away and go out for breaktime.

That must be why Kesha ran out of the classroom so quickly – she wanted to talk to Zara. About me? Maybe.

That would explain why they went all the way over to the football pitch. They didn't want me to catch them. That's why they were hiding behind the tree – so that I wouldn't see them when I came out.

3 Kesha doesn't like me

They don't want me to hear them talking. Kesha is asking Zara to be her new best friend.

Zara is saying, "Oh, I thought you were best friends with Carrie?" And Kesha is laughing and saying, "What, boring stupid Carrie? No way. She thinks I'm her best friend but I never really liked her."

Now they are laughing at how stupid I am to think someone like Kesha would ever really like someone like me. Boring, stupid me.

Kesha isn't normally mean. She's always nice to my face so why would she do this behind my back? Unless she's only pretending when she is nice to my face. If she doesn't like me anymore, she should just tell me.

I don't care.

I've got lots of other friends. I don't need Kesha. Lots of other people like me. In fact, everyone likes me.

Maddy and Sunita both really like me. I'll choose one of them to be my best friend, now that I'm not friends with Kesha anymore. Sunita, I think. She's nicer than Maddy and she has a puppy. Maddy won't be happy. But she can just play with Zara and Kesha.

Kesha!

Why doesn't she want to be my friend anymore?

We were friends yesterday. And the day before that.
And every day for two years. Ever since we found out our
birthdays are on the same day.

We're supposed to be having a joint birthday party at
Jumping Jacks in two weeks' time.

She won't want to do that now. The party will
be cancelled. My birthday will be ruined.

4 The girls don't like me

What's this? I think it's Tilly's glove. She must have dropped it. She'll need it if she wants to make snowballs or build a snowman. Where is Tilly? I can't see her anywhere. Is she avoiding me too? And Izzy … I can't see her either. Is everyone avoiding me?

Oh … hang on … there they are. They're not avoiding me. They're just building an igloo. Phew!

"Tilly! I found your glove!" I shout to her.

She doesn't look up.

"Tilly!" I try again.

Oh … I see. It isn't her glove. She has both gloves on.
It must be someone else's. But why didn't she reply?
Why did she ignore me? Izzy is ignoring me too.
And they think it's funny. They're laughing. I bet they
know about Kesha hating me and are laughing
at me while they're pretending to build an igloo.
That's so mean. I was only trying to be kind.

Whose glove is it then?

Ah ... It's Shayna's. She's making snow angels with Kitty and Grace and I can see that she only has one glove on. Her other hand must be freezing!

"Shayna! I found your glove!" I shout and wave the glove at her.

She sits up and looks at me. She looks confused.

I point to the glove I'm holding and then I point to her. Then I point to the glove again. She realises it's her missing glove and gets up and runs over to me.

"I found it on the ground," I say to Shayna.

"Thanks," says Shayna.

She takes the glove from me and goes straight back to Kitty and Grace.

5 Nobody likes me

Charming! They carry on making snow angels. I'd quite like to do that. It looks fun. Why didn't Shayna ask me to join them? Maybe Kesha told her not to let me play because I'm boring and stupid. Kesha probably told all the girls – Maddy and Sunita and Tilly and Izzy and Shayna and Kitty and Grace and Uma and Suri and all of them – because now that I think about it, everyone is ignoring me. I've never been ignored so loudly in my whole life.

Kesha and Zara don't want me to have any friends at all.

And look! Now Kesha is telling Charlie!

And Charlie will tell Tayo and Evie and Zac and Eli and Katie and Ola because they are all playing football together right now.

And now nobody likes me. Nobody. I have no friends.

Ms Ali comes over to me.

"Carrie, are you all right?" she asks.

No, I'm not all right. Nobody likes me.

"You look sad," says Ms Ali.

"I don't have anyone to play with, Ms Ali," I say.

"Who do you want to play with?" asks Ms Ali.

"Kesha," I say, "but she wants to play with Zara,
so she obviously doesn't like me anymore. Then she
told Maddy not to like me. And the other girls.
And the boys. And now nobody likes me."

"Kesha actually did that?
You heard her?" asks Ms Ali.

"Well … no … I didn't hear her. Or see her.
But I'm sure she did it," I say.

"Carrie, sometimes our thoughts run away with us, and
we think things are really happening when they're not.
It's just our brains playing tricks on us," says Ms Ali.

Great. So now even my own brain doesn't like me.
And Ms Ali thinks I'm imagining things.

"We all overthink things sometimes, Carrie," says Ms Ali. "We just have to realise when it's happening and try to stop it, but that can be tricky sometimes."

I'm so stupid. I think I'm going to cry.

"I can't help it, Ms Ali," I say. "One thought turns into another and before I know it, everything is racing through my head. And then I get sad or angry or scared and I can't tell what's real and what isn't. I hate my brain!" I say.

"Go easy on yourself, Carrie," says Ms Ali. "Take a deep breath. Count to ten. Talk to someone about how you are feeling."

26

I take a deep breath and I count to ten in my head.

I guess I do feel a bit better after talking to Ms Ali.

"Here comes Kesha, Carrie," says Ms Ali. "Why don't you talk to her and sort it all out."

Kesha! Finally!

She's coming to talk to me. She'd better not be coming to tell me she has a new best friend and doesn't like me anymore. Then I really will cry!

6 Kesha likes Zara

"Carrie! Carrie! There you are! I've been looking for you all breaktime!" Kesha calls out.

I try to be calm and not get angry but it's really hard, because I know she's lying. She wasn't looking for me, she was with Zara. So I was right all along and Ms Ali is wrong about me imagining things.

"What's wrong, Carrie? You look angry," says Kesha.

I am angry. I feel like I'm going to explode.

"I saw you, Kesha. With Zara," I say.

"Yes, I asked her if she'd seen you come out to play yet, but she hadn't," says Kesha.

"So why didn't you leave Zara and look for me somewhere else?" I ask.

"I was going to, but she was nervous. She wanted to play football with Charlie and the others, but she was too shy to ask," says Kesha.

"Oh," I say. I didn't know that.

"She plays in a team every Saturday. She loves football," says Kesha.

"Oh," I say. I didn't know that either.

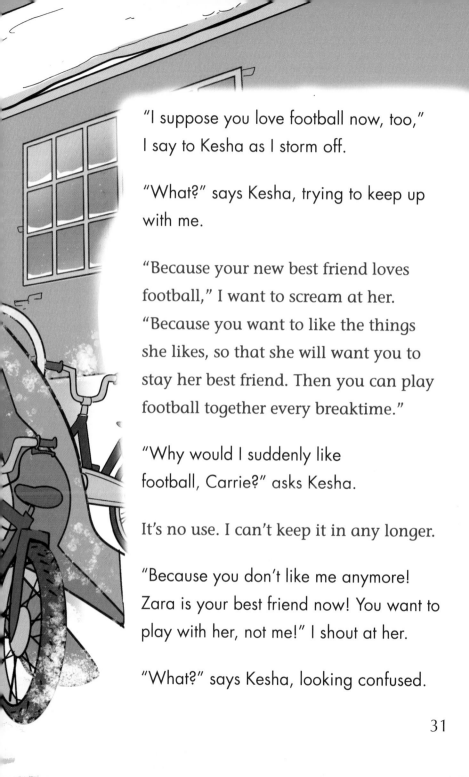

"I suppose you love football now, too," I say to Kesha as I storm off.

"What?" says Kesha, trying to keep up with me.

"Because your new best friend loves football," I want to scream at her. "Because you want to like the things she likes, so that she will want you to stay her best friend. Then you can play football together every breaktime."

"Why would I suddenly like football, Carrie?" asks Kesha.

It's no use. I can't keep it in any longer.

"Because you don't like me anymore! Zara is your best friend now! You want to play with her, not me!" I shout at her.

"What?" says Kesha, looking confused.

"Don't act like you don't understand," I say. "You didn't wait for me to come out of the classroom because you wanted to ask her to be your best friend and you didn't want me to hear or see. You asked her if she liked me and she said no. I saw her shake her head! Then you both laughed at me."

"I asked her if she had seen *you*," says Kesha. "I told you that, Carrie."

"Then you went to tell Charlie that you didn't like me," I say.

"I suggested to Charlie that Zara would be a great striker in their football game," says Kesha.

She is lying. She must be lying, mustn't she?

"And you told Sunita and Maddy too. And they told all the other girls. All the boys know too. And now nobody likes me! They are all ignoring me," I say.

"When did I do that, Carrie?" she asks me, still confused.

"When you … umm … when you – "

7 My brain doesn't like me

I stop. I realise that the only person I actually saw her talk to was Charlie. And I suppose that could have been about Zara playing football, as she claimed.

I didn't actually see her talk to Sunita or Maddy.

Oh dear. Have I got this all wrong? Could Ms Ali
be right? Have I been overthinking everything?

What did I actually see? What did I actually hear?
I think back through everything that actually happened
and rerun it in my head.

35

"You ran out of the classroom after Zara," I say.

"I ran out to play in the snow," says Kesha.

OK, well, I suppose that could be true.

"You and Zara were behind a tree," I say.

"The football pitch is next to the tree," says Kesha.

Yes, that is true.

"You and Zara were hiding," I say.

"We were just standing on the other side of the tree from you," says Kesha.

Well, yes, I suppose they were.

I may have misunderstood everything I saw.
I had one scary thought and I've let it
grow and grow and turn into my
worst nightmare. None of those
things really happened.
They were just
in my head.

The boys weren't talking about me, they were talking about Zara playing football.

The girls weren't ignoring me, they were just playing with the snow.

One bad thought became another bad thought, and then that became an even worse thought.

It's just like Uma's snowball, rolling down the slope.

It gets bigger and bigger and faster and faster until it's so big and so fast I can't stop it anymore. I didn't even realise I was doing it. It all made perfect sense at the time. Ms Ali was right. I am overthinking and I do have to realise when that is happening.

8 Everybody likes everybody

"I'm sorry, Kesha. I thought you didn't like me anymore. I don't know why," I say.

"Don't be silly!" says Kesha. "You're my best friend!"

Phew! Everything is fine. Although I think I need to learn to recognise when my thoughts are running away with me. And talk to the person I am overthinking about – check what's real and what isn't. That will help me to stop it.

Ms Ali blows her whistle and we're about to go back
inside when I see Zara running towards us.
She looks muddy and out of breath.

She is probably coming to thank Kesha for suggesting
to Charlie and the others that she could play as striker
in their game. Kesha is really nice, and good at helping
people and being friendly.

I suppose I am too, really. Zara might want to be my
friend too. All three of us could be best friends together.

I wonder when Zara's birthday is?

If it's soon, she could share our party. But … she'll want a football party and I want trampolining. But I'll have to agree because she's one of my best friends now. I hate football parties and now I have to have one.

"Thanks, Kesha!" says Zara. "I scored twice!"

She will definitely want it to be a football party.

I don't have any football boots. I'll have to ask for
a pair for my birthday, when I don't really want them.
I want rollerblades. Mum won't buy me both. It's too
much money.

Oh.

Hang on.

The snowball is rolling down the slope again! I must
stop it before it gets out of control. Why can't snowballs
roll uphill and get smaller? It's really hard to make my
thoughts go backwards but I have to do it.

"Wow! That's brilliant!" Kesha tells Zara.

"When's your birthday, Zara?" I ask.

"22nd March," says Zara.

"Mine is next week. So is Kesha's," I say. "Do you like trampolining?"

"I love it. Next week! You're so lucky. Mine is exactly eight weeks today," says Zara.

"How many days is that?" asks Kesha.

"Eight times seven is ... 56!" says Zara.

Oh. 56. Not 58, like I wrote in the times tables test. Got that one wrong. And probably all the other times tables questions. Urgh. I'm so stupi–

Wait! The snowball is rolling AGAIN! I need to stop thinking and say something.

"Oh … I put 58 as the answer to that question in the test," I say.

"It doesn't matter. It's just one sum," says Zara. "You probably got all the other sums right, Carrie."

"Yes," says Kesha. "You're really good at times tables, Carrie."

That's kind. They're both kind to me. I should be kind to myself too. I'm not stupid, I just got one sum wrong, that's all. THAT'S ALL!

The snowball effect

Kesha is hiding
from me.

Kesha doesn't
like me.

Kesha and Zara
are best friends.

The girls are
ignoring me

Kesha is telling
the boys.

The boys are
laughing at me.

And now nobody
likes me.

Ideas for reading

Written by Christine Whitney
Primary Literacy Consultant

Reading objectives:

- make inferences on the basis of what is being said and done
- ask and answer questions
- predict what might happen on the basis of what has been read so far
- discuss and clarify the meanings of words
- discuss the sequence of events in books and how items of information are related

Spoken language objectives:

- participate in discussion
- speculate, hypothesise, imagine and explore ideas through talk
- ask relevant questions

Curriculum links: Science: Animals, including humans: recognise the impact of diet, exercise, drugs and lifestyle on the way bodies function

Word count: 2999

Interest words: avoiding, overthinking, misunderstood

Build a context for reading

- Look at the front cover, the illustration and then the title. Encourage children to share their understanding of what the book will be about.
- Read the blurb on the back cover. Ask children to suggest what is happening in Carrie's mind. Do they have any advice for her?
- Encourage children to share their experiences of friendship.

Understand and apply reading strategies

- Read Chapter 1 together. Ask children to explain what Carrie believes has happened to Kesha by the end of this chapter.
- Continue to read together up to the end of Chapter 2. Ask children to explain why Carrie thinks that Kesha would prefer Zara to be her best friend.
- Read Chapter 3 together. At the end of this chapter, Carrie says, *My birthday will be ruined*. Encourage children to explain why she thinks this.